The Telephone

Please Let It Not Ring

Smita Ghosh

ISBN 978-93-5458-931-7

Published in India 2021 by Pencil

A brand of

One Point Six Technologies Pvt. Ltd.

123, Building J2, Shram Seva Premises,

Wadala Truck Terminal, Wadala (E)

Mumbai 400037, Maharashtra, INDIA

E connect@thepencilapp.com

W www.thepencilapp.com

Author biography

Smita Ghosh lives in Odisha, India with her husband, an exceptionally perfect dog, and an attack cat.

"The Telephone" is Author's first book of the series "Horror Adventure"

Before she started writing , Smita got a graduate degree in Bachelor in Arts. After that. she did a handful of clerkships with some really important people who are way too dignified to be named here.

She was a Accountant for a while. She now writes full-time.

CONTENTS

Epigraph

"There is something at work in my soul, which I do not understand."— Mary Shelley, Frankenstein

Preface

"THE TELEPHONE" BEGINS WITH THE STORY ABOUT A GIRL NAMED ADITI KHANVILKAR. SHE HAD SUPER EXCITED AS SHE GOT A NEW JOB. SHE FELT LIKE NOW SHE WAS MATURED ENOUGH TO TAKE HER DECISION.SO SHE BOOKED A BEAUTIFUL NEW APARTMENT AND HERE SHE MADE A BLUNDER.EVERY NIGHT THE TELEPHONE RANGS AND TELL SOMETHING TO ADITI...

TO KNOW WHAT HAPPENED TO ADITI PLEASE READ THE BOOK AND ENJOY....

HAPPY READING.....

Life is what happens to you while you're busy making other plans-----S.Ghosh

THE TELEPHONE PLEASE LET IT NOT RING

Aditi Khanvilkar was ecstatic about the move. She had recently switched to a new job, and now she had a beautiful new apartment. For the first time since leaving home, she felt like she had some handle on her life.

The very first room she had rented when she had moved out of her parent's house was a seedy-looking, beat-down coffin; with barely any space for a kitchen or study table. That was all she could afford at the time. Now, two years later, she had moved up the corporate ladder and earned enough to move out of that death trap, and into something more resembling a home. Aditi was happy.

The intercom telephone rang at about 2.00 in the morning. Aditi had been sound asleep. Exhausted by all the unpacking and organizing, she had lain on her bed and had instantly fallen asleep. The ringing woke her up in a daze of confusion. She dragged herself from her bed and half stumbled, half walked to the living room, where the intercom was affixed to the wall.

"Hello?" The static echoed in her ear. "Hello?" Nobody answered. Agitated, she hung up and dragged herself back to sleep.

By the next morning, Aditi had forgotten all about the midnight blank call. It had been another bone-crunching, tiresome day. She had organized the bedroom, the kitchen, run a couple of cycles of laundry, and hung them up to dry. She had taken a few days off from work to get settled into her new home; she just hoped she would be able to get it all done in time.

Late at night, the telephone rang again. Sleepily, Aditi walked to the telephone and stared at it in frustration. Who was calling at this godforsaken hour! The clock on the far side of the living room wall blinked at 2.00 A.M in big red digital letters.

"Hello?" Static. Garbled sounds. "Hello? Who is it?"

She felt like someone was speaking, but the sound of the static and garbling was so loud that she couldn't hear anything else.

"Sorry. I can't hear you." She dropped the receiver on the phone and walked herself back to bed and presently to blissful neverland.

She was heading out for her morning walk the next day when she remembered the midnight call and halted at the watchman's cabin.

"Uncle Ji, could you please give me the extension for the intercom in my flat?"

"Flat no. 204?"

"Yes please."

"I am sorry madam Ji, that phone is not working," said the watchman.

Aditi looked up from her belt pouch, where she had been hunting down her headphones. "Excuse me?"

"Yes, madam Ji. The owner lived for a very short time and when they left they asked for it to be disconnected."

"What? But it is not disconnected." She laughed hesitantly, unsure whether this was some sort of prank. "I got a call last night."

The watchman looked at her quizzically.

"But madam ji, that cannot be. See here…" He removed a huge old - fashioned register from under the desk and turned to a section that listed the names of all owners against flat numbers. He ran his finger down the list eventually stopping at Flat no. 204; where the entry was followed by a big dash. Blank.

"What does that mean?" Aditi asked, pointing to the blank.

"Madam, it means that either the number was disconnected and a new number has not been assigned, or the night watchman didn't know the number or forgot to write it."

"Maybe that's it," she said, slightly relieved. "Could you please check in with the night watchman when he comes tonight?"

"Yes, yes madam. Don't worry, I will do that."

The telephone and the conversation with the watchman slipped from Aditi's mind until she was woken up yet again, in the middle of the night, by the loud ringing of the telephone. She sat bolt upright in bed. The phone rang for what seemed like an eternity and just as she had decided to go and check, it fell silent. She let out a breath she didn't know she had been holding.

A second later the phone started ringing again and her heart jumped up from her chest and lodged itself somewhere in her throat. Chest heaving and heart-thumping, she padded down to the living room and picked up the receiver with trembling hands.

"Hello?"

Static. She waited in the garbling silence, straining to hear.

Suddenly, through the intervening space and time, she heard a rasping voice that pierced her being like a crystal knife of horrifying clarity. HELP ME!

She dropped the receiver and stumbled away from it. She hugged the opposite wall and stared at the dangling receiver. Loud sputtering static issued from the speaker. The horrible voice faded away. She mustered herself, approached the receiver with caution, and placed it on her ear. Silence. The telephone seemed to have died. She gulped soundlessly, her mouth suddenly parched. She replaced the receiver and picked it up again; there was no dial tone.

Aditi couldn't sleep that night. The ragged, coarse whisper grated on her eardrums and echoed in her mind. When she closed her eyes, she felt certain that the voice on the telephone was still calling her. Help. Help. Help.

The next morning, she almost ran down the stairs and pounded on the watchman's desk.

"Did you find out what the problem is with my intercom?"

"Arre madam ji. Like I told you, it is out of order." The watchman said in an exasperated tone.

"And like I told you," Aditi leaned in closer to the watchman over the desk and he backed up in surprise. "It is NOT out of order because someone is calling me!"

"But that is not possible!" The watchman's tone changed from exasperation to irritation.

"Okay. Dial my phone. We will check right now."

"Madam, you are not understanding what I am saying! There is no extension..." The watchman faltered at the look that Aditi gave him and backtracked quickly. "But I guess we can dial the old extension just to check."

Some unknown feelings did belly flops inside Aditi's stomach as she watched the watchman dial i204. Presently, he handed it over to her and she held it close to her ear, her heart banging against her rib cage.

Nothing.

"It's not ringing," she said mechanically.

"That's because that line is dead madam like I already told you." The watchman took the receiver from her frozen fingers with the vindictive look of someone who had just proved his point.

"But .. but..." She stammered and looked around wildly. How could this be? The phone HAD rung and she HAD heard that voice. Was it a dream?

"Okay." The watchman raised his hands in a placating gesture. "We can talk to the phone company and call someone to check it out if that's what you want madam ji."

She nodded absently.

"Yes okay. Yes please do that."

Aditi returned to her silent apartment, befuddled and dazed. She sat in her living room and stared at the telephone. The ringing of her mobile phone jerked her out of her reverie with a jolt. How long had she been sitting here? She stood up from the couch and her legs cramped horribly. The phone call was from her office. They had called to enquire when she would be able to recommence work. She fabricated something about not feeling well and needing a few more days and hung up. She ordered lunch from swiggy and after a long, aimless walk outside, she returned to her empty apartment and dozed off for the entire afternoon.

A youngish man came in the evening, accompanied by the watchman. He tinkered with the phone and wires for a few minutes and declared, to everybody but Aditi's relief, that the phone was in fact completely dead. The watchman gave Aditi an - I told you so - look of self-importance and she felt a sudden red hot rage erupt inside her at this smirking individual.

She managed to keep it inside and smiled petulantly back at him. She declined to get the phone connected; it was giving her enough trouble while it was disconnected. She was barely home, and if someone wanted to call her, they could call her on her mobile.

As the sunset outside, Aditi sat up in her bed fully dressed and began her long vigil through the night. She had turned on every light fixture inside her flat. If someone had stood outside on the road and looked up, her flat would have glowed like a jewel in the middle of the inky blackness of the midnight sky. Several times during the night, she jerked awake after having dozed off and imagined that she had heard the dreaded ringing of the telephone within the confines of her mind.

She had been dozing off again when the clock struck 2.00 A.M and the apartment was filled with the screeching of the ringing telephone. Her entire body erupted in gooseflesh and her skin turned clammy with the sudden cold sweat. She walked stealthily towards the door and grabbed the keys as she made a silent but mad rush to get out of her apartment straight to the desk of the night watchman. She reflected that the lump in her throat was a scream she was barely managing to repress.

Aditi banged on the security cabin's window a couple of times before the night watchman started awake.

"What? What is it?"

"I want you to come up to my room right now!"

The watchman blinked at her; taking in her mussed-up hair, the sheen of sweat on her forehead, and the panic in her voice.

"What happened madam Ji? Nobody got in. Is everything alright?"

"No! Come with me!" She turned around and dashed upstairs, trusting the watchman to follow her; and feeling slightly reassured as she heard his footsteps behind her.

By the time they reached the open door of her apartment, the telephone had stopped ringing.

"What is it, madam?" The watchman rushed past her and cautiously entered her brightly lit apartment, looking everywhere at once, his baton held at the ready to fight off the intruder.

"The phone..." Aditi gulped. "The phone was ringing."

The watchman lowered his baton and looked at her, completely befuddled.

"Madam, that phone is…"

"Dead!" I KNOW! She screamed. "It is disconnected! Out of order! And IT WAS RINGING!"

There was a sudden rattling and creaking behind her and both of them turned abruptly to see the next-door neighbor's latch open. Faces were peering out at them in the gloom.

"What is the matter Ramkishan?" asked the owner of the flat next door. "Nothing sir Ji." The watchman walked over to the door. "Everything is okay. Madam just had a bad dream."

He looked at Aditi daring her to challenge him. She lowered her head, there was no point in countering or arguing now, so she nodded.

"Yeah, I thought I saw someone inside my apartment. It…It must have been a nightmare."

She stood in the middle of her living room as Ramkishan bade goodnight to the neighbors; back to the safety of their own homes and beds, where there were no ringing telephones.

He returned to her. "Madam, are you okay?"

Aditi heard the genuine concern in his voice.

"I am sorry Ramkishan Ji. I shouldn't have woken you up."

Ramkishan accepted her apology with a nod. "It's okay madam, that's what I am here for. Please lock your door. I will get back down."

After locking up, Aditi spent the night sitting upright on the couch by the telephone. It did not ring again that night.

When the phone rang at 2.00 A.M the following night, Aditi sat on the living room floor and let it ring. The house was ablaze with lights, and she sat through the infernal ringing, her body growing colder and her breathing becoming ragged.

There was a strange pull to the ringing. It called to something deep inside her until nothing remained but a persistent, horrific, almost cloying mantra of - pick it up... pick it up. No matter how much she restrained herself, she found her being gravitating towards the ringing and her body almost being dragged to the telephone, against her frantically screaming mind and heart.

Help me...HELP ME...HELP...KILL...ME

The rasping, dead voice on the telephone reverberated through her relentlessly.

Sometimes the words were almost human, and sometimes the static mingled with death-defying, ear-piercing screeches of extreme pain and horror; it was like listening to the amplified sounds of a nail being scratched over a blackboard, repeatedly.

It gritted over her psyche, scratching out her nerves and senses, leaving them red, raw, and bleeding in its wake.

Sometimes there were words in the unearthly jumble of screams that had no meaning or context; like the sound, you hear if a cluster of loose teeth is thrown into the meat grinder. The soft tearing sounds of the screaming throat, punctuated by the jarring, tinkling of breaking enamel.

HE...KILL..   AARE...COME...
SAVE...YOURSELF...

Aditi stopped sleeping at night; she couldn't. With the sickening anticipation of what was coming at 2.00 A.M hanging over her like the rotting, sulfurous odor of burning flesh, it was impossible for her to close her eyes and lose herself in the blessed relief of the darkness; only to be violently dragged away from it by the sharp, painful hooks of the ringing telephone, piercing deep into her organs.

Most nights, she hunched over in a corner of the living room, her hair wild, her eyes bloodshot; blabbering senselessly, constantly until the ringing of the telephone stuffed her words back inside her mouth and she felt like she was gagging on her own vomit.

She slept fitfully during the day. She stopped going to work. Her nightly encounters with the paranormal phenomenon of something she could not describe or even comprehend made her jumpy and extremely frightful. Every night as the clock struck 2.00, the telephone started ringing, and her heart stopped beating.

Aditi was so petrified by what she heard on the other end of the line, that she became extremely suspicious of her mobile phone as well. One day she took her hairdryer and smashed it into her mobile phone. She sat in her corner in the living room and brought down the hairdryer again and again on the already cracked screen of her mobile phone. She screamed as she crushed the pestilential device, and laughed hysterically at the mutilated remains. This phone at least will never ring again, she had made sure of it.

It was only after the sudden and tragic demise of her mobile phone, that she realized that she did not have any means of contacting anybody else. She did not have numbers written down. What would she do if she needed help? HELP ME… KILL ME… the words rang through the chambers of her mind, and she laughed ever more maniacally at her own stupidity.

Aditi ventured out of her apartment the next day. With her phone smashed, she realized in hindsight that she couldn't order food. So she unearthed a bag from the pile of haphazardly strewn utensils and potato peels in the kitchen and decided to buy some groceries.

The sunlight hit her like an avalanche; paralyzing her with its warmth. She blinked and squinted in the bright afternoon light as her eyes adjusted to the world outside. She joined the small queue outside the milk center in her colony. As she waited for her turn, avoiding the gazes of the people around her, she saw a large billboard, off into the distance, advertising Aarey Milk.

Aarey.. Aarey... Aarey... the word rumbled through Aditi's mind as she stood frozen in place, her eyes wide and her mind selecting and discarding words to illuminate a connection that eluded her. AAREY...AAREY... She kept staring at the billboard, and people behind her in the line, pushed past her, muttering, scowling, wrinkling their noses at her disheveled appearance, and shaking their heads. AAREY...AARE? AARE!!

Her heart thudded to a stop within her chest and all the breath seeped out of her. Could it be? Someone else pushed past her, elbowing her in the chest, and she started out of her reverie. She stared wildly around, unable to focus and determine where she was... why she was. How? Her eyes snapped back to the billboard of their own accord and it all came rushing back to her. Frightened out of her skin she ran out of the line.

She spent the next half hour trying to flag down a rickshaw, to no avail. Until finally, just as she had started to give up, one came around the bend and stopped beside her. She glanced at the middle-aged, round, and stocky driver.

"Aarey?"

"Aarey Milk Colony?" The driver asked.

Not knowing if that was where she was supposed to be headed, Aditi nodded timidly.

"Bahut door hai madam," the driver deliberated. "Very expensive. 500?" He enquired, an eyebrow raised.

Aditi opened her purse and handed the 500 rs note to the driver.

He smiled broadly at his luck and turned down the FOR HIRE sign.

"Let us go madam!"

Aarey Milk Colony*, Goregaon. Aditi stared at the empty streets, shadowed, gloomy under the canopy of the trees that stood resolutely on both sides of the roads. There was a spooky, disquieting stillness to the air that made her hair stand at the back of her neck. Her mind urged her to get out of here as soon as possible, while her gut told her she had come to the right place.

"Where should I drop you madam?" The driver looked at her in the rear-view mirror.

"Here is fine," Aditi said, indicating the crossroads at the next corner.

For a few minutes she stood at the street corner, and watched the tail lights of the rickshaw shrinking slowly and disappearing into the gloom. Now what? She thought to herself. She walked further down the street and looked about her for some kind of street sign or marker. She felt an odd sort of clarity; it was like waking up after a long, horrendous, terrifying nightmare and realising that it was just a nightmare. She tried to recall the broken fragments of words she had heard on the telephone, and attempted to make some sense of them.

She had been walking for about fifteen minutes when she felt the now familiar pulling sensation somewhere within her. She stopped and took great, heaving breaths to calm her nerves that had gone on hyper-alert. She took a few steps forward and felt that wrenching again in the pit of her stomach.

It hit her suddenly, that this feeling was horrifically similar to the dreadful pull she felt when the telephone rang. She took another step forward, and the feeling clenched harder on her intestines and pulled her in the opposite direction!

Aditi turned and took a few steps in the opposite direction, and the clenching eased; confirming her worst fears - it was leading her to wherever she was supposed to go. But what was it! Aditi screamed into the recesses of her mind. She followed the pull and walked with increasing apprehension towards it.

Ten more minutes of walking, led her to the driveway of a huge old Victorian-style bungalow. She gazed at the white picket fence and the red shingled roof. There were two-three cars… Jeeps?… standing in the driveway. The house looked like something out of a dream, picturesque and well cared for.

Her heart slowed as she realized that she had been expecting to be led to a broken down, haunted old and abandoned mill, or something akin to a house on a haunted hill. This was not so bad. The pull in her tummy increased to an urgent, dull dread. Yes, this was the place. Not knowing what to do, Aditi rang the bell.

The guard at the security gate did not allow her to enter and repeatedly told her to shoo away. But Aditi persisted and rang the bell again and again, and refused to be shooed until she met the owner. The guard went inside the house, reluctantly and muttering about layabout, good for nothing beggars. To her surprise, he returned presently and led her inside.

The owner, Tarun Kishore Verma, turned out to be a police officer. He was well-spoken and seemed genuinely concerned about Aditi's state. He introduced himself and invited her to sit on his living room sofa. He inquired politely whether she was alright and if there was anything he could do for her. Aditi, who had been living an increasingly strained existence, broke down under the careful and gentle ministrations of this kind stranger.

Weeks of pent-up frustration and pain overwhelmed her increasingly building a sense of caution and fear. She howled out loud and began to cry with great, heaving screams and sobs. She ended up telling Mr. Verma everything. Beginning with that first night when the disconnected telephone had rung, right down to the moment she was led to his front door by an unseen tether and forced to press on his doorbell till she was admitted.

Mr. Verma listened to her, never interrupting her, merely nodding at the appropriate places to indicate that he was listening. After she was done, Aditi sat on the sofa, looking out of the large french windows of the living room, at the dying light of the day.

Mr. Verma's house servant brought them two steaming mugs of tea, and he insisted Aditi drink up before continuing the thread of the conversation. She felt marginally better after the tea. The slow burn of fear crept up inside her as she contemplated going back to her apartment with the infernal telephone.

"Aditi," Mr. Verma called her to the present in a gentle, almost lulling voice. "Thank you for telling me everything. I cannot imagine how difficult it must have been for you to be living under such ghastly strain for so long." He visibly shuddered.

"This is my Police ID," Mr. Verma extended his badge.

Aditi took the card and saw a small picture of him dressed in khaki uniform, along with the details of his post and station. She handed it back and nodded for him to continue.

"I am showing this to you, because I cannot in good conscience ask you to return to your apartment, where you have been so obviously distressed."

Something akin to hope fluttered somewhere within her heart.

"So, I request you to stay here for the night, relax and recuperate. And tomorrow we can go about discussing what is really happening and how to deal with it. How does that sound?"

A fresh bout of tears seized Aditi and she blurted out her thanks and how grateful she would be if she could just spend one night here, away from the telephone.

"Of course. Of course." Mr. Verma patted her awkwardly on the shoulder, his own shoulders sagging with obvious relief. He told her to wait in the living room, while he went to prepare the guest room for her.

Aditi stood up and faced the last glimmers of the setting sun visible through the french windows. She closed her eyes and breathed deeply, smiling slightly at the thought of having one night of uninterrupted sleep.

A sudden crack jolted her and she looked around wildly for the source of the noise, her heart hammering in her fingertips. The lights flickered and a chill crept over her as she moved away from the open windows and towards the hallway that led to the inner rooms.

An old-fashioned landline telephone hung on a peg on the far wall, and her feet moved her towards it. It seemed to be a souvenir or antique; the ones Aditi remembered seeing in old Hindi movies from the 70s. It was in pristine condition except for a few places where the gold paint had chipped and fallen off. She touched the faded spots and felt the granular texture beneath, the paint seemed to have been gouged out. She stepped closer to look at a spot on the receiver that looked sort of dull and black when the phone vibrated in her hand.

She tripped backward in shock, dislodging the receiver from its place, and collided with a small stool that held an ornate vase. The stool wobbled and before she had any time to react, the vase tipped over and shattered, spilling fake flowers, plastic leaves, and decorative pebbles everywhere.

Mr. Verma came rushing out of the hallway and looked around wildly before spotting Aditi, lying on the floor. He knelt down and grasped her shoulder with alarming fierceness.

"What happened Aditi? Are you alright?"

"I…" She faltered at the sudden steel in his otherwise mellow voice and was then brought sharply to the present by the loud static emanating from the dangling receiver.

"The phone!" She screamed and raised a finger towards it.

Mr. Verma looked from Aditi to the telephone and then back again, obviously confused.

"What about it Aditi?" He asked his voice returning to his previous polite tenor.

"Don't you… Don't you hear it?"

"Hear what?"

Aditi stared at the telephone in utter horror. The static spewing out from the receiver rose to a deafening crescendo and the space around her condensed to a strange kind of vacuum. With an ear-splitting roar the receiver spat out one single word before it went deathly silent.

RUN!

Her stomach did a somersault and bile rose up in her throat as the world spun and the void enveloped her.

Aditi woke up in darkness. She wiggled around and managed to free herself from the tangle of bedsheets around her. She was dripping with sweat. For a moment she couldn't place herself and stared around, trying to recollect the shadowy space around her.

Then her eyes adjusted to the gloom and she realized she must be in the spare bedroom at Mr. Verma's house. She stepped down from the bed onto a soft, spongy sort of a carpeted floor, and moved around the room trying to find a switch or... something.

As far as she could make out, the room was fairly small, with just the bed and not a single piece of furniture. The wallpaper was strangely soft to the touch. She brushed her fingers along the walls as she circled around the room. Presently she bumped her knees into the edge of the bed and her fingers scraped at something installed on the wall next to the bed.

She drew her fingers away as if burned; it was a telephone! She sidestepped and walked backward, trying to put as much distance between herself and that device, as she could. She backed into the opposite wall and clung to it, staring into the darkness, in the direction of the telephone.

No. She closed her eyes. She will not be cowed again.

Please let it not ring, she pleaded. Please!

No! It's not going to. You are not there, this is not that phone.

Please let it not ring.

But then, what had happened with that other phone in Mr. Verma's living room.

That phone had rung.

Please let it not ring.

Aditi slid slowly down and sat hunched over the strangely carpeted floor and hid her head within her arms. The chill came over her, almost welcoming her body, greeting, and caressing it like an old friend. No. No. No! Her heart thumped in her ears, and her closed eyes reverberated with the rhythmic beating. It was coming, she knew it.

The telephone rang.

Aditi screamed at the far wall, tears spilling out of her eyes, a dribble of snot dangling at the end of her nose. She pelted towards the phone and battered at it with her bare hands, banging, pulling, and scratching at it, trying to pull it apart and destroy it.

The ringing came to a sudden halt as her hand knocked the receiver from its place and the room filled with the loud, sputtering sounds of static.

She continued to pull the telephone from its roots. She pulled out the receiver from the phone and threw it aside. The garbling and sputtering grew louder until it filled all the empty space within the room and forced open her tightly closed eyes and pushed past her tightly shut throat. She banged her head on the dial piece in a last-ditch attempt to dislodge it from the wall.

There was a loud crack and with an overpowering stench of iron in the air, blood spurted out from her skull and streamed down her eyes. The receiver vomited a few gasps of indecipherable static.

HE IS COMING!

The words stabbed at Aditi's resolve and she stood stock still as the static died. The lights went on suddenly and her pupils constricted and then dilated as she took in the room around her. The walls, floor, and even ceiling were padded. The padding must have been white at some point but now stood frayed and patched and crimson with large splatters of what could only be blood and tissue.

With a jarring, sucking sound a door popped open. Mr. Verma stood in the shadows, his eyes glowing out of his haunted, almost demented face.

Aditi saw with gut-clenching horror that he was holding a syringe in one hand and a chainsaw in the other.

"Hello, Aditi. I see you are awake."

Aditi screamed. Her voice transformed into a low, guttural, primal shriek as her throat tore open with the strain and blood started spurting out from her mouth. She stumbled forward, gagging at her own blood and snatched at the receiver now lying silent on the floor.

"HELLO!" She croaked into the receiver, her eyes growing wider with fear, at the approaching figure of the monster with a chainsaw.

HELP ME! PLEASE! SOMEBODY!... HE WILL KILL ME!. HELP!

In a different part of the city, about twenty-five kilometers from the Verma residence, a different telephone started ringing.

Glossary

1. Ji: Suffix that is used to denote respect. If we want to give respect to someone then we put 'Ji' after their name like 'Uncle Ji' or 'Madamji'.

2. Bahut door hai madam: It is a very far madam.

List of Contributors

Author-Mrs. Smita Ghosh

Editor-Mr. Sumit Mishra

Notes

Aarey Milk Colony, Goregaon East is a luscious green spot in the city of Mumbai, which also happens to be one of the most notoriously haunted places. By day, it's a pretty spot to take a walk-in. But by night? Well, let's just say you'd do better to avoid it. For years, people have reported incidents from the Aarey Colony road. People often see the lone figure of a lady in white following cars, while drivers have reported seeing a similar figure following them through their rearview mirrors, and no matter how fast or slow they go, the lady in white always maintains exactly the same distance from them. Others have reported seeing a lady covered in injuries weeping on the side of the road, who runs after their car, screams at them to stop for her, but disappears when they are brave (or stupid!) enough to do so.